~

A Mouth of Vowels

~

1366Books

Ontario

Canada

ONTARIO ARTS COUNCIL
CONSEIL DES ARTS DE L'ONTARIO
an Ontario government agency
un organisme du gouvernement de l'Ontario

Canada Council for the Arts
Conseil des arts du Canada

~

A Mouth of Vowels

~

sophie anne edwards

1366Books

Guernica founder: Antonio D'Alfonso
General editor: Michael Mirolla
1366 Books editor: Stuart Ross
Interior design & typesetting: Stuart Ross
Cover & 1366 logo design: Underline Studio
Author photo: David Wiewel

Guernica Editions Inc.
1241 Marble Rock Rd., Gananoque, ON K7G 2V4
2250 Military Road, Tonawanda, NY 14150-6000 USA
www.guernicaeditions.com

Distributors:
Independent Publishers Group (IPG), 600 North Pulaski Rd., Chicago IL 60624
University of Toronto Press Distribution (UTP), 5201 Dufferin St., Toronto Ontario M3H 5T8

First edition. Printed in Canada.

Library of Congress Control Number: 2025943565

Library and Archives Canada Cataloguing in Publication

Title: A mouth of vowels / sophie anne edwards.
Names: edwards, sophie anne, author.
Description: Series statement: 1366 books ; 4
Identifiers: Canadiana (print) 2025024540X | Canadiana (ebook) 20250251485 | ISBN 9781771839990
(softcover) | ISBN 9781778490002 (EPUB)
Subjects: LCGFT: Novels.
Classification: LCC PS8609.D87 M68 2025 | DDC C813/.6—dc23

For my mom, Dany (1941–2025), who inspired my love of books and who remembered, even when she couldn't remember much, that I had a publisher. And for Emilie, my golden thread.

"All living is listening for a throat to open..."
Claudia Rankine

1 There were no drum rolls. Sulphurous lightning lit the darkness.

2

3

2 The centre of the cake falls. The baby bites her nipple.

3 Apples, cat food, appointment w DS, refill tire.

I needed something

for

me. 4

5

6

4 A door slams in Abc, Elsewhere, at the same time as a door on River Road, Ontario. Are they equally blue?

5 What is the price of a belly filled with foot?

6 Statistically speaking, there are no statistics. If something is continuous. If the sky opens like a cervix around midnight. It has happened already. She speaks in letters rather than words, hands out multiple sets of vowels.

7

7 A yellow door and red thunder rumble at the same time. Docs this make nipples more sensitive? Can a cake rise from deformed words? She adds powder for extra protein, washes the spoon twice.

888

8 A calculation is a breath expelled.

After eight weeks of silence
a foetus begins hearing sounds
within the body 9

10

11

12

9 The baby pats her mother's breast. The mother washes the cake and stacks water on the shelves.

10 Pears.

11 Stairs.

12 After eighteen weeks of silence, a fetus gathers sounds lapping within the lake of the womb. Do the unfurling ears of a gestating baby hear the sound of two small hands clapping?

13 (8 months of silencing + 9 months gestating in silence do not equal 17 months.)

14 15

14 One arm holds what is remembered without mercy and the other weighs what is forgotten deliberately.

15 Is a core an apple?

16

17

16 An apple tree is a library of limbs.
17 The young apples are hard green satellites. She hears them orbiting in the crackling blue night.

18

19

18 She listens for the words that crawl down the walls. If the baby nurses four times in the night, will the gathered sounds unravel?
19 The invisible borers are boring under the bark. The grooves may or may not kill the tree, depending on how many woodpeckers drill holes through the bark. She lies in the silver dark and listens. She is sure she can hear the borers because the flesh of a tree and the flesh of a woman are the same distance from the sky.

20

20 Under the yellow paint of the bedroom, old boards calculate the capacity of dry rot. If one board rots faster than another, is the house ninety or one hundred footsteps from a squirrel's nest? Is a house with yellow paint a nest or a murmuration? She hears the breeze enumerating leaves outside the window.

five

five

five

five

five

21 She walks in the middle of the road. A man, who will gather apples from her yard, raises his fingers from the steering wheel in a nod. Unthreaded birds fly upward from her raised palm. If she counts steps, the baby will not slip from her arms, through the metal girders, into the river. The girders are mouths that call her name.

22 The baby picks at a mole sprouting on her neck. If she counts her steps, a tapping drip, will the apples ripen on a Monday or a Tuesday? If she walks in the middle of the road, she will be invisible.

23 Words tap onto the melting street. Her footsteps, armfuls of vapour, count the hours. The hours may or may not weigh the same as a nodding baby. When the baby naps sixteen instead of nineteen minutes, she finds her way home.

ou are [25]

You a

ou are [24]

You ar [25]

26

27

24 The birds gather her steps for their nests.

25 Each step repeats *you are you are you are you*

26 *you are you are you are you*

27 *are you?*

26

1 8

14 6

21

9 13 22

5 16

11

28

30

23 4

24

10 25

31

20 2

17 12

19 3

18 27 28 29

15

7

28 One.

29 Two.

30 Three.

31 At twenty she loses count. At thirty-one she starts again.

32

33

32 There are twenty-two steps from the yellow bedroom to the front door. The light under the door of the blue bedroom is a red fire. If his words crawl like worms under her skin, will a cake rise when a hunter knocks on a door?

33 A yellow bedroom can become a blue bedroom in the space of two red-handed minutes.

35

34 35 34

35

34 If her heartbeats are cross-sectioned, there is an equal chance she will be thirty, five, or a blackbird singing in a pie.

35 She pats the baby's belly five times to understand his hidden words.

must tell me
thing. I will find
out if you don't. There
are ways. You need to
prove yourself. You are
crazy.
Get up off the floor.[38]

36 A twenty-pound note is hidden in the bear. If the bear is stuffed, will she be caught in the crosshairs?
37 Where CW equals the number of holes and JL is the number of words that leak from these holes, she will empty at the rate of five clouds per hour.
38 The holes in her skin are rings that orbit her body. The holes spell *husband*.

39 The formation of a particular cloud confirms that if she holds the baby too long, the holes in her body will replicate onto the baby's skin.
40 The inverse holds true.

41 The baby is a nectar-seeking bird. The cries are midnight, 1 a.m. 2 a.m. Three. Four. Five.

42 Her breasts are blue-veined moths that cipher the weight of purple. The baby's belly is a red apple. Blue and red do not always erase purple.

43 Six is not a number.

44 Twelve stairs up do not equal twelve down. She counts steps + breaths like white noise. If a woman, pregnant on a street in Abc, Elsewhere, will feel a midwife's fingers spreading her cervix, how many apples will fall in the moonlight?

45 She thinks, *If I slide into the river with the baby, we will both sleep awhile.*

47

47 48

46 50

48

46

47 48

50

48

49

46 She thinks, *I will hold this baby until there are no more holes.*

47 She thinks, *The holes will multiply the night eight times.*

48 She thinks, *If the holes in my skin are multiplied by the number of woodpecker holes drilled in a tree, my skin will no longer contain me.*

49 She thinks, *The baby will be my skin.*

50 She thinks, *No, my skin is the baby. Or my baby's skin is an apple. Or the baby should not be my skin, but if a baby comes from your skin, is she your skin?*

51 If a sapsucker's tongue contains an anticoagulant,

will his words disintegrate?

52 Wasps and a drunken bear hover under the tree scented with rotting apples. If small pound notes are hidden in a bear, and a passport is locked in a desk in an office in Abc, Elsewhere, will skin translate the watermarks staining four fat loaves of fishes?

53 The baby's moulting skin is an iridescent murmuring.

54 She listens to tendrils reaching through air.

55 She is sure she can hear the roots growing because the sap of a tree and a cervical plug are the same weight as water spilling into a lake.

56 If her cervix does not efface and the midwife must run her fingers around the lip of her, and the pain spreads like lightning and she is falling into dark that sounds like sulphur from a fired gun, can a tree hold two hundred apples?

57 She holds her breath for 35.2 seconds. Will a baby breathe evenly in the granular days and blue nights, if a placenta weighs more in one hand than in another?

58 Are apple blossoms an index of moonlight or the number of trees awakened in the night?

ill be a terrible mot
o you have any idea how terrible you a
o one should allow you to have a b

59 The baby rolls her head unevenly around the cervix. The mother ties her palms to a flock of birds feeding on burnt orange ash berries. If the cervix is a half-moon, will the baby be a girl? The midwife measures the cervix with the sound of an opening wing. If the midwife's fingers span the width of a cervix, will blackbirds fly out of the pie? Will the pastry sprout o's? The fingers of the midwife spreading open a cervix voice a loosening of questions.

your passport after the wed 60

No, yo 61

give me the money you ear 62

60 Apples wrapped in newsprint will sometimes become green-blue powder. If forty-six apples are wrapped in paper and stacked gently in a cardboard box stored in a cold room for 5.8 months, how many apples remember the moment they germinated from hard black seeds?
61 If she bites an apple, and the flesh is rotten and her fingers push through, has she pulled the trigger? If the apple looks firm and red in her hands, and his hands make her flesh soft and rotten, will the moon efface?
62 His words are sticky holes. His hands, embossing machines. Her flesh is a function of rotting apples multiplied by the number of days of rain in September. His words raise a pattern of consonants on her skin.

63 The worms aren't noticeable until the apple is bitten. In the night she listens to the thud, thud, thud of red, dropping to the ground. Her breasts swell like twin moons, drip in anticipation of the baby's need.

64 Sometimes the bruising of an apple browns the flesh but not the skin. Will his fingers sink into her soft flesh if he touches her arm, raised and gesturing toward the tree? The hunter places a pile of soft apples 100 metres from a stand with a clear shot. The deer follow the scent of apples winding a path through tamarack and cedar. If a doe drops her head to a pile of apples and a woman does not see the rot under the flesh before she bites the apple, will the deer eat well? Is the moon a cervix?

65 If a doe approaches apples rotting in a field while a cake falls in an unevenly heated oven in a house from which apples have been collected, will the baby cry in the night? If the baby soothes herself by crawling to the breast and the mother doesn't waken, does the crying count? Does the deer look up first?

66 A deer will be shot cleanly through the lungs, visible sound becoming visible scent. The hunter remembers the colour of her shirt but not how much pastry clung to the edges of the pastry cutter.

67 If her belly is smaller than expected and a doctor in Abc, Elsewhere, rewrites the due date, will the baby be a boy?

68 (Visibility is a function of skin holding shape like the scent of apple blossoms.)

three

one

two

seventy

69 The glasses whistle.

70 One.

71 Two.

72 Three.

73 (Invisibility is a function of water falling through a sieve. Invisibility, a sieve, does not calculate the thrumming of wings lifting from a tree.)

74 The knocking of the door doesn't stop.

75 She prunes the cake. Pages bloom from cracks in the tree trunk. Into the borer holes she plants sheets of paper torn from unread books. The baby suckles her finger. Her hand is an index. She writes a series of checks and balances made out to the groundhog drilling holes in the grass. The missing pages sprout propositions.

76 Pound notes can sometimes equal two half-formed portraits.

77 The knocking is a flight of birds.

78 If a cake 3,322.86 kilometres away from a street in Abc, Elsewhere, bakes at 350° for 45 minutes, and she looks up at a hunter casting a shadow in a honeyed doorway, will the baby be gathered up with the apples? The baby bites her nipple. Her hand, lightning, strikes like thunder. A cheek brightens like an apple.
79 The knocking is knocking.

80

82

80 Are steps toward a door a baby's cries? Are steps away from a door a mother's mouth? Twelve steps forward are a flock of birds. The sudden uplifting of wings from the ash tree is a heart. The feet at the door lift and settle, lift and settle. A grouse runs three times around the base of the cedar tree. She tucks the baby's cries, which have startled the grouse, into the pastry. Her heart thrums in her throat. Her throat may be a grouse or the flight of birds. Twelve steps backward are a closed throat.

81 Nine months of gestation sometimes carries the same scent as wings thrumming across the sky.

82 The door is a knocking against the hand.

84 83

85

86

87

88

89

83 She weaves broken sentences in strips across a pie.
84 Weft.
85 Warp.
86 She peels the apple, the soft flesh of his neck. Water flows over the edge. Worms wriggle under the skin. Apple. Corer. Dish. Oatmeal. Peel. She removes each mirror from the house but one. One may be necessary. It is necessary to not look. He holds her head to look.
87 Five.
88 Seven.
89 It is necessary not to look, but the mirror is an echo of eyes.

lean

gainst

the

wall 90

91

92

90 The knocks at the door accumulate. She hides the baby in the drawer, tucks the pastry roller under her arm. Gestures. The apples begin to rot under the tree, soft intermittent thuds like her memory.

91 She looks at the words, rising like a moon, a pastry of letters that spell *lean against the wall.*

92 She folds the baby in the pastry and unlocks the apples. *Take as many as you like.* She is not sure she has spoken out loud. The hunter offers a twenty-dollar bill. The hunter gathers small red moons in a cardboard box. The hunter looks at the door closing, a mouth of fingers, a month of moons. Her shirt is an apple skin.

93

94

93 A flock of grackles flies from the tree, a thousand heartbeats that smell of earth, a dampened fire. Does the baby disappear when she turns toward a blooming network of bird trails?

94 The baby's belly is a small red moon grafted to grackles lifting from a tree. The baby's heart beats twice between each beat of her heart.

her I

her I her

ill her aw I wil

tak her a ill

awa

he

95

96

95 She threads the fallen apples to the tree. In response to a question he will will not she drops a skein of woven threads from her mouth take.

96 The baby is tethered to the mother by silk threads spun her away by the light emitted by a dozen bees.

97

98

99

100

97

98

99 Mercy is sleep in the shape of a cookie cutter. Sleep may not be a mercy.

100 A swing with a girl at the top of a green hill is a closed door. Her feet are fragile wings.

ow what you're thinking. I can loo
d know what you're thinking. Don't tr
ide it from me. You will tell me eve
ings have a way of comi 101

will kno

102

101 Is a good girl a bird? Is a wing a feather?

102 She counts his breaths. If he can't hear her heartbeat and a bear leaves its scat in the grass while a mirror records his voice, a tree may or may not produce apples. How many breaths is a bird? How many exhalations an exit? Will the bird expire while she counts exits?

103

will kno 104

103 The worms migrate through the basket of rotting apples that is her flesh. If a doctor redacts two months and her belly is a swollen arc and a plan is a laced trail, will a cake rise? Will ribbons spool from her mouth?

104 The baby's opening eyes gather spools of light. She is a library of unauthorized books.

105

106

107

105 The baby's rippling flutters are slow braille under the skin of her belly.

106 A slowing baby is a flight risk. A travel plan. A hand searching for a thrumming heartbeat on the tight drum of a belly.

107 The customs officer notices that her face is a flight of birds. Small stones fall through her stitched lips onto the counter.

108 109

108 The borers are invisible in the visible dark.

109 Does one invasive combined with one introduced equal four or five seasons of held breaths? The moonlight is cradled in the boughs, which are bated breaths. If she does not breathe enough times for the baby and the trees succumb to the tunnelling borers, and a plane falls from the sky, and all the doors along the street are cavernous stains, will the baby grow one or two feet?

110

111

112

110 She counts her steps in the night. The baby gathers her breath. There are twenty-seven steps to the front door.

111 This is not the same front door. This may be the same front door or it may be a calculator.

112 When she counts backwards from zero, she is hidden again.

113

114

115

116

117

113 If a hunter stands in her honeyed doorway and gestures to a tree dropping apples to the grass, will worms drill into apples? Will the baby stop crying? She fills the cradle with the baby's cries and tucks the baby in her apron pocket. If she and the baby are constellations, will there be four or five dozen apples per box? She swallows thunder.

114 *Please,* she said.
115 *Yes,* she says.
116 *Help yourself,* she says.
117 *I have nothing.*

118

119

120

121

118 She may have said, *I have nothing left.*

119 The hunter sends her words back on a twenty-dollar bill.

120 The hunter hears her open her mouth but can't see what she is saying.

121 *It is nothing,* she said. Or maybe she said, *I am nothing.*

122

123

124

122 *Help yourself,* she says.
123 *Help yourself,* she said.
124 She hears the fluttering of echoes. She's not sure if she has opened her arms in a gesture or stocked water on a shelf.

125

126

127

128

129

125 Sometimes green apples do not turn red before they fall.
126 Sometimes night is not night but a humming.
127 Sometimes skin is a spoken word.
128 Dusk is a twilight ribbon. The stars are succulents. When a deer and her fawn flatten grass in their sleep while a hunter rests in a chair facing the window, watching the night and a woman and a baby dream green dreams, twelve steps divide 3,322.86 kilometres into evenly paced slices.
129 She bakes a square from his jacket into the cake. (Sometimes a square is a burnt circle.)

knock [130]

knock [131]

130 In the night she holds her palms out the window to the twittering stars. If a deer flattens a grassy area and a hunter twitches in his sleep, will the baby sleep through the night? Will the red and yellow leaves drift back up into the branches?

131 The apples fall to the ground from her overfull arms. The baby suckles an apple. Pastry rises from the ground around her feet. The worms are drunk with the scent of the baby, round as an apple.

132 Branchlets sprout where there are cuts. If a branch is cut and the wood burned, will the moon rise each night?

133 The ringing phone is one hundred apples thrumming. She hangs up three times and hooks the receiver on the fridge door. *Patty cake, patty cake,* claps the baby.

134

135

134 If the mother gazes into the baby's face, a skein of fine threads, will water run from her palms? And if she snuggles chin and nose and clasps the small face in her threaded hands, will the grosbeak hanging upside down outside the window eating mountain ash berries tie her fingers to the clouds? Will a tree full of berries sound the same as one rotation of the moon?
135 Twelve bars of moonlight write migrating verses on the wall.
136 The baby claps her hands and gazes into the mother's face, a waning moon. If the baby suckles chin and nose and clasps the mother's face in her small hands, will the mother's hands rethread themselves?
137 Their skin is a collection of water droplets.

138

138 Two doe and their three fawns drink at the shoreline. One raises her head. They eat small moons from the water. The doe's milk is warm under the blue-veined sack of her skin. The deer retracing their steps in a daily circuit calculate the waxing of the moon. The brown scent of the deer collects under the apple tree in the night. The mother hums the lines of browning apples while counting the baby's digits. 1, 2, 3, 4, 5, 1, 2, 3, 4, 5, 1, 2, 3, 4, 5, 1, 2, 3, 4, 5. The next number is not an exit.

139

139 Fold the apple tree. Fold the wood. Trim the towels.
140 The folded towels are sleeping birds. The baby hums. If a baby hums and claps while her mother's hands are folded in the towels, will the worms crawl out? Does one song equal a dish of parsed fingers?

141 Fold once, twice.

unbuckle 142

143

144

145

142 A mirror is a repeating witness. A mirror is a thousand birds tied to apples turning in the sun.
143 The white sink is a cold band of lightning ringing her mooning belly.
144 There are eight steps from the sink to the bedroom. The floor may be a fire, an open pit, 3,322.86 kilometres, a rope.
145 (Look.)

e has studied, he says. It is here in this bo
ws him. You must foll
says. You owe me. 146

147

148

146 Each step is an eye.
147 How many acts balance words that have been spoken, words that haven't?
148 *Tap tap,* echoes the mirror.

149

150

pick 151 up 152

Now 153

Close the 154

155

156

149 Does a balance balance what cannot be seen with what is deliberately shown?

150 five, six

151 pick

152 up

153 seven, eight

154 close

155 the

156 (A closed gate is a weight.)

157

158

157 The hunter tips four boxes of apples in piles at the intersection of two deer paths. The paths are blackened lines. The hoofprints of the deer sink into the soft wet earth. Water collecting in the divots is a collection for the silver moon. A puddle is a migration of orbits. If a mirror mirrors what she tries not to see, while a hunter recalibrates his scope, will the bear hold enough pound notes?

158 She peels his neck, which is the skin of an apple.

159 After twenty-eight weeks, a floating fetus with budding ears swallows the vowels her mother swallows. Sound filters from beyond the warm lake. *Gurgle gurgle,* says the baby.

160 *Gurgle gurgle,* says the warm lake.

161

ant you to

162

little girls 163

161 She closes the book of matches three times. It is a book of fire. She swallows the lightning. Twelve struck matches do not equal nine months. Twelve photos of a baby do not equal twelve equal payments.

162 When both sides of a scale ignite fires in the walls, respiration is miscalculated.

163 When a man studies the weight of words, the words are a weight.

164 Fill once, twice.

165 166

165 The placenta is a blue-veined planet. The midwife uses four fingers to spread open the cervix, a collapsing orbit. She guides the baby with two hands. Her two hands unravel a thin umbilical cord wound four times around the baby's neck. The birth attendant has ten long fingernails that cannot relieve the black-and-red pain that stitches her back. A hunter fills two dozen casings with gunpowder. Is a deer a needle pulling thread?
166 She buries the upturned lily pad under twelve handfuls of dirt.

167 168

167 The baby looks up from the bassinet into the open sky. The baby opens her mouth and cries and cries her cries. The bassinet is an open sky. The sky is a bassinet into which her cries tumble. The cry is the first cry that cannot be soothed because the sky is open and the expanse a violet crackle that does not gather her cries. The baby sees infinity for the second time. (Infinity is a gathered breath.)

168 Hold once, twice.

169

170

169 She prunes the apple tree. Branches lie tangled in the grass. Where there are cuts, shoots shoot from the tree. She grows extra limbs to hold all the unhealed cuts.

170 She listens to green crawling through the window, a weaving of breathing lines. The bees buzzing in the blossoms are yellow threads of light. The green trees tint the yellow walls green. If she stays in the middle of the room, they will not fall into the garden. The boys calling *car* will not float into the clouds. The holes of the screen will balance the weight of the pollen gathered on the wings of one hundred bees.

171

172

173

171 If a single bee lands in three hundred blossoms and a hunter flicks on a light at 5:02 a.m., will the baby sleep for one or two hours? Will her limbs hold? Is a screened window a printing press?

172 *Take as many as you like,* she says, opening her arms.

173 *I have nothing else,* she thinks she says.

174 gai

175 agai

174 She ties the bill to a musical note and tucks a robin's song into her wallet. There are no bears under the tree, but she threads money and grows extra eyes, extra ears. Her ears are tunnels.

175 The baby blows raspberries, which the mother hangs from the doorknob. She closes the door four times. The sound of a door closing once is a rumble. Closing five times is a sky breaking open. She watches the hunter gather apples. 1, 2, 3, 4 boxes. 1, 2, 3, 4, 5 apples. Start again. 5, 9, 11, 8, 10, 7. She loses count at 2:29.

Start again.

Start again.

176

176 Hydro. Groceries. Phone bill. Don't phone Bill. Mash baby food. Words fly out when she opens her left palm. Worms continue to burrow through the apples. Her other hand opens and closes, opens and closes, catching light that thunders blue. The apples are worm-bored. The crows circle their eyes on the humming apples rotting beneath the tree. When a house in Abc, Elsewhere, fills a room on River Road, crows caw a line of curling apple skins.

177

178

179

180

177 *Caw caw.* She scrapes consonants into the compost bin for the crow.
178 When she peels the apple and a single long peel curls away from her knife, will the meaning of nested cutlery become legible?
179 *Baa baa,* says the baby. She threads her little fingers through her mother's hair and clasps her mother's thumbs, which may not be fingers but a row of knives, or rings of apple peels.
180 If the moon rises at 8:49 p.m. and the baby nurses only three times in the night, will the letters tumble out of her mouth in an orderly fashion? Will she sleep in the bed she has made?

ive m 181

wipe the blood from the sheet 182

oven 183

184

152

186

187

181 Each morning she blows on the baby's stomach to release the worms. The worms she has gathered have spread from her skin to the baby. The baby's fluttering hands spin strings of light that float around her mother's head, a cocoon.

182 She opens her mouth, releasing a buzz of bees. She tucks in the butter and spreads the sheets.

183 A bun in the oven is a bird in the hand.

184 The heating oven ticks. The baby crawls backwards.

185 Ten. Nine. Eight.

186 Plant fall bulbs. Baking powder. Jacket.

187 Tisket. Tasket.

188

ort back if you're a good gi

189

189

188 A door is a mouth. Apples fall from her open mouth.
189 His suits are shadows. Her passport is confiscated. 3 jacket buttons x 7 suits in a line do not equal 21. The arms flap up, releasing a flock of words. She is a startled bird.

y should I take you to see the midwif

?

190

191

192

190 An apple a day has kept the doctor away. She counts feet in the belly. 7, 5, 4, 3, 2. Do seven good deeds equal a passport? A good girl is not an apple.

191 One.

192 A quieting baby is a conference of clouds.

od girl

good gir 193

ood girl

good g

good 194

oo

od g

gi

193 Blackbirds spin songs between the branches, an alphabet of dropped notes germinating in the grass. Their shadows, as they flit across the window, are flickering messages. A flicker flits through the trees. The baby's eyelids flutter a coded response. The mother catches the red flickers on her tongue, translates them into an archive of beads. The mother's eyes flicker with dreams the baby will later remember.

194 In the spilling quiet of the evening, she clasps the baby's bundled body.

195 The quiet hours gather on the hunter's orange coat. His skin is insulated with needles dropping from the trees. If a hunter quietly follows a deer's tracks and clear glasses are stacked on a pine-board shelf she has mounted on the wall and the wall is painted yellow, will the deer eat twelve or thirteen apples before looking up? If she doesn't look up, does the mirror count breaths? Will the board hold the weight of 365 nights of sleepless dreaming, without warping?

196 Steam rises from the hunter's open thermos. The fallen leaves are coloured storms. If a blue umbilical cord is wrapped four times around a baby's neck and it is so thin it pulls away from the placenta and a deer produces milk under her velvety skin, does one pound of yellow equal twelve cut branches? Is yellow a mercy? Is a deer a midwife? Is an umbilical cord the beginning or the end of a sentence?

197 Her body is a weight of bodies. The weight of one body is a smashed plate. The weight of multiple bodies is a murder of crows. If a belt no longer closes the pants over her swelling belly, will the shirt be wide enough to hold the weight of his sentences? Is the thunder of silent hands balanced by the lightning of a girdled belly?

watch h

198

199

198 An exit is sometimes translated through flesh. The light crawls along her curled fingers, curled along the floor. If light weighs like bars, will the door stay blue? 1, 2, 3, 4, 5. The next number is forgotten. Six is a fire. Six is a swing rising into the sun.

199 His words conduct the shapes that gather sibilants in the pathways under her skin. His hands spell out, *Repeat after me.* She is a reader of braille raised on the air.

ear you 201

200 His words are red pistons that puncture the skin of the sky.
201 *Je te plumerai.*
202 She lies in the liquid air of the night. Blue fills her veins. She is a weight sinking. The baby is a weight on her chest breathing, breathing. She counts their breaths rising and falling. The baby's cries are the tight rings of a tree, ridged bark ringing her body, two, three, four, five. If blue is a number, will the hours in the night divide thirty by a dozen apples?
203 She sweeps up dead sentences, taps the glass four times.

204 If she forgets what he remembers and her pulse is a diving bird, will what he deliberately remembers balance what she unwillingly forgets? Will what he wilfully forgets outweigh what she unwillingly remembers?

205 What he wills her to remember outweighs the number of pounds a bear can hold.

206 (There are no stories when the mind must be an open book.)

uld you 207 walk u 208
look ook th
is a fire 209

207 He knots her voice with the threads he cuts.
208 She threads two streams of thoughts. She feeds one through her violet mouth. The other she hides in the thread he unthreads from her. She learns to think in weavings. She taps Morse code onto her belly.
209 *Tap tap,* taps the mother.

e on your belly. 210

210 If she closes her eyes, will the baby be a girl?

211 Five.

212 Four.

213 If it's a boy.

walk up the hi
again 215

214 Can she translate the sweetness of an apple if she doesn't know the varietal?

215 Jack and Jill go back up the hill.

would you walk up
look don't that is a fire

at the door

look look down of the
[216]

Look [217]

216 would you walk up
don't look don't look that is a fire
217 like me the rest a look of winged questions
at his hands are her hands
flap a harvest look

look up

see her there

you see her

I know you saw

her

218

218 A swing carving lines in a blue sky is a pendulum, carving chain links into her repeating eyes. As long as she looks, the swing will stay empty. If she looks away, the swing will not be swinging.

219 She holds her breath so he cannot see the memories stitched to her tongue. Stitches can be ropes. She has two threads of words, one that worms deeper into her veins, the other translated by his hands. The words she has given him have become a fire.

220 Her mouth is an open sore, a cored apple.

the sink hold the cold
look open your eyes hands
the sink i sink the sink i am
cold words a river
his words are
that spin the sink is
It
you have to make it
up to me 220

221 If a woman is released into the dark night with no money and no papers and he drives away in a car that is an accelerating wish, will the worm routing in her belly grow antennae? If the car is a decelerating sentence, will her arms encircle two or three cold moons?
222 Is a fetus a divining rod?

223 The cake sprouts the blue shirt. Plaid spools from her open mouth. If each square is a kilometre, how many worms are in her head? The baby is a ridged apple tree. The baby is barking. The house is a milestone, or is it a millstone?

224 Sounds slip from her lips while a cake bakes unevenly in an oven eighteen steps from a blue door. If the hunter's fingers touch the blue veins on her hand where a twenty-dollar bill unfurls, will bees rise stinging from her skin?

be

o

bend over and

over

225 If her cervix is an unthreaded moon, will a uterus fall from the body? One. Two. Three. She threads labia to mouth so the body does not fly skyward. She sews more hands to her arms to hold her body together. The womb and throat stitch one blue line running from seven to thirty-seven.
226 Missing vowels do not add up to repeated steps.

227 Each step is a repeat.
you are you are you are you are
are you are you are you are you are you are you
six eight
228 His twelve words and her twelve words do not add up to two full sentences.

Get u p off the floor

re crazy.

ou are c

You are 227

229 Get up the floor gets up the floor get up

One. Two. Buckle my

230 The bodies on her body are a chorus of thunderclaps siphoning her breath.

231 (Memory is a multi-limbed fire.)

pick up

232 Does a body rocking back and forth on the floor, its skin a skein of prickles, twelve finger lengths from a crack of light, weigh the same as a skein of sky unfurling from an apple press? Is an apple a bruise? His words backstitch her veins. The listening baby gathers threads.

233

234

oy I want you to have an abortio 235

saw you looking at him 236

237

233 Two. Three.

234 If it's a boy.

235 Five. Seven.

236 Lower the temperature, the shelf, the photograph, the arm, the limb, the teddy bear, the window,

237 your eyes.

238 The doe threads her way through the trees.

239 Where there is one, there is another.

all. Lean agai
wall. Lean against the wall. [240]
Lean against the wall. Lean against the wall. Lean against the [241] wall.
Lean against the wall. [242]

240 Two boxes of apples tumble against each other in the bed of a half-ton pickup.
241 Half walking, she crabs to the bed. He has cleared a corridor in both directions. The words she has spoken are twisted between his fingers. Or is it the words she hasn't spoken? The hunter sits at the centre of the corridor. The deer stand is a small planet.
242 If she reduces the sugar in the cake she is baking while a deer nurses a fawn in the yellow morning in the whispering rain, will the walls ignite? The fawn draws threads of milk from the doe.

rn back up the hill. Can you see her knicker 243

243 If the hill is a return and he asks her to watch, will fruits of the loom become waning moons? If one hill becomes two, will the 243 typeset steps carry forward thirty years? A swinging swing is a bated breath.

Trouble and strife: wife 244 245

No is not an answer. 246

247

244 Trouble and strife: wife
245 Apples and pears: stairs
246 The buzzing in her hands is a closed razor. A razor in the hand is a calculation of a bee loaded with pollen and the weight of eleven humming days. If water droplets gather under his chin where a razor might be, will the cake divide evenly?
247 She stuffs her mouth with shards. She feeds small bones while his words vibrate through the skin of a belly.

248 If one choice weighs more than a box of apples and the other more than a pot of sauce made with apples from the same tree from which a hunter gathers red moons to bait deer, will the apple tree grow an even number of branchlets? Will a mouth full of worms form words? If both choices are equal to a row of dark suits, how many apples can she hold in her arms?

249 *you will you will you will you*
will you will you will you
will I will I will
I will
will I?

250 The blue-and-orange-flecked tie he knots round his neck drags her wingless body through the door of a train. Will the baby pulsing in her belly flip one or three times in its saline lake?

251 Silence in a belly is hammered braille.

lk back up the hill. Tell me what you saw. 253

252 The apples fall from her opened hands. *Thud thud thud.* Where they fall, worms gather.

253 The midwife lifts the baby in a square of fabric tied to a handheld scale.

254 An apple a day is an apple.

255 A day is an apple.

256 Apple day.

257 Apple.

258 Turn.

259 Over.

260 The knocking continues knocking. The knock is a twenty-dollar bill. *Take it,* the hunter says, gesturing. Jill runs down the hill.

261 Between the stars and the dew on the grass is a harvest of ungerminated lines.

262 *Take more,* she gestured to the tree.

263 *It's nothing,* she thinks she said.

264 Cardboard boxes soft with damp sit in the grass. The hunter looks at the doorway. Berry and apple seeds fill the bear scat. He fills the boxes with browning moons. It is not spring that excites a man but fall. If she doesn't look, he will not see her. A burned pot always burns in the same spot. If the hunter sees her and her hands are birds, will the pot burn? Is a burn an apple? Will the boxes remember the number of apples they held?

265 *I saw nothing,* she might not have said.
266 The palms of her hands are flames.
267 The bear has a hole where her hands came free.

269

268 At 2 p.m. each afternoon, the baby breathes on the mother's blue-veined breasts. They sleep in a yellow room while apples sweeten in the chilly air. She has a head full of ears. She wakes to the suckling baby each time a bat orbits the house. The doe and the yearling are bedded under cedars, twining underground. Their bodies leave a circle of indentations in the grasses.

269 *Hum hum,* hums the baby.

270 Is a core an apple?

I'm counting 273

271 (Apples sweetening in the cool evenings are a calculation of eternity.)

272 The gentleman goes riding, riding.

273 Eleven.

274 Twelve.

275 Thirteen.

276 The doe pawing the ground with one of her two front hooves catches the scent of apples. A pile of apples blinks in the moonlight. When deer wind through the paths that wind through cedar and poplar and the scent of rotting apple threads from the centre of the path where the hunter has tumbled them from four boxes damp with dew, and the apples were gathered from a house with blinking windows, will twelve jars of applesauce snap within five minutes of being pulled from the water bath? Two. Three.

277 The number of times the hunter has seen the woman weighs less than a voice.

278279280

278 Damp is sewn into the hunter's skin where the square was baked into her pie. (Sometimes a pie holds all the words.)

279 The lake enters the kitchen through a silver thread. If she can hold the water in her arms, the sky will douse a green hill with blue-scented breaths.

280 If she holds the moulting crayfish in her arms and descends the stairs once with each foot, the kitchen will not be a dank mouth.

not know what or how long.

do not know what or ho

I do not know w

281 A small foot in the belly is a bird in the hand.

282 Twelve blackbirds baked in a pie.

283 Do twelve taps tapped by a foot from within a warm sack in the belly equal twelve foot taps outside a belly?

284 Can twelvefold jars of canned applesauce hold the breath required for an open throat? If she cans thirteen jars instead of fourteen, will the voice tremble? Will words thread from her mouth in even lines? Will worms exit wounds?

285

286

holds her head to lo
Look, he sa
Look.
he sink
is cold on her bel
e pain is hot 287

285 When an oven heats evenly and a woman's cervix thins unevenly and she is floating into a blue that tastes like a closed tunnel, will the crow hop five or seven times in the grass? Is the baby's blood a ribbon of half-risen beats?

286 If she holds the baby long enough, will his words leak out? Will the baby translate her mother's love—a constellation of regenerating organs—into twenty toes and fingers?

287 She peels her skin—the full draft of his words. Consonants fall from her mouth, a murder of crows.

ill take her from you.

288

289

288 If a six-month belly becomes five with a doctor's note and a plane thunders silver threads, will the alphabet reorder?

289 *You do not look six months pregnant,* she thinks she hears. Do clasped hands around a belly erase a doctor's lie? Will a flight be safer than a tree of falling apples? Thicker than a closed door? Is a recalculation a lie or a waiting room? A silver flight is a thread, is a belly, is a fire.

290

4

36

290 If a pie is cut into fine slivers and she holds her palms outward from the bottom of an open window before the rain, will deer align along their well-threaded path? Is a path a pie? Nine slices of pie and four plates do not equal thirty-six hours of labour.

291 The womb is the only organ with two kinds of muscle. If one muscle contracts longitudinally and the other gathers the rinds of apples, is a womb a galaxy or a forest?

292 If she forgets where she is, if there might be here, or rather here might be full of there, and the muscles of her uterus cannot contract, will one thousand bees drop from the sky?

293 She repeats, *The cord, the cord,* while the midwife's fingers unspin the pulsing thread. If the midwife reverses the sentence that is a twisted cord, will the baby grow more after or before her fingers push through the soft flesh of the apple?

ust watc

hildren i

yground. Report back

want to kn

u saw. Get in be 295

294 Jack and Jill went down the hill. Jack walked back up. *Open your eyes.*

294.5 If she opens her eyes, will the swing be empty?

295 If her eyes are lidded, he cannot see the birds flapping in her head.

296 Nine.

297 Nine.

298 What one is required to see.

299 Report back.

300 An empty swing is a breath.

I have studied this. 301
I don't know how long.
I'll tell you when.
You just have to keep proving
doing what I say. 302

303

301 If a car speeds through a tunnel wide enough for two vehicles, one of them a truck with a window overlooking a car with a woman wearing a plaid skirt and she is soft and pale like the moon, will her scent release the debt he has stacked? A speeding car may not have enough speed to unthread the needle that is his silence. Will a string of words release a debtor?
302 An unsigned debt sometimes outweighs an assigned debt.
303 (Sometimes a debt weighs more than the debtor.)

Steam rises sweat look at him

I saw you looking clouds

beads I saw you I told you

304 Her belly, a liquid moon, touches the floor. Sky spills from the spaces between the threads that thread her mouth. Her hands are tight apples.

305 If his voice spreads through her belly, will a boy become a girl?

306 How many vowels does her debt weigh?

bloom what time to not look

treacherous
a sky of is it Mr. Wolf? 307

307 Steam rises of sweat look at him
I saw you looking clouds
beads *I saw you* *I told you* *you are*
bloom what time. *to not look* *treacherous*
a sky of is it Mr. Wolf?

308 Beside the bed is an orange-covered book. She records the blooming of the belly. Unravelled words backstitch the space between visible and invisible. Between the stitched lines is an invisible weave.

309 Her lungs are compressed. She sleeps sitting up, bile drowning her throat. He ties her tongue to his fingers. The window lays yellow bars along the blue-covered bed. She practises breathing without breathing. When a woman is calibrated for a slight drift, can a breath recall the length of a rifle?

310 She slides her loose words across her belly.
311 The cells that exchange between the body and the baby do not balance. Does an apple balance the seed it produces, the seed that produced it? As her throat closes, does the baby's open? Does the subtraction of mouths equal the months of dividing cells? Does a swallowed tongue become a throat in the belly? A handful of eyefuls?
312 She walks up and down the stairs twelve times during 5.5 minutes. Her ten fingers sink into the yellow walls. Sometimes a baby's breath is a father's hand at the throat. Her skin prickles. She is pinned to a dozen migrating birds, a constellation stretched in the sky. The baby's cries are constellated backstitches.

313 Her alphabet ends at b.

314 B is an apple rotting on the ground in a pile of rotting apples. She covers the words in her head with twists of apple skins.

ose your mou

315

315 If the room and the house and the sidewalk and the street are pins, does a 750-millilitre jar of unfiltered honey suspend illusions? She is a moth pinned to the bed by an alphabet of errors. When a woman eating cereal in a blue room crunches too loudly, a pillow is not an exit. She is a thousand shards in a silence that burns heartbeats. Her tongue is a pin cushion.

316

316 If a man collects a junior alphabet of knickers and an attic is an archive of thunder, will the sidewalk open mouths or doors? If a man opens drawers while threading telephone wires, is a collection of knickers an alphabetical stairway or a vacuum?

317 Dark suits hanging in a line are a hung jury. The dark suits tailor accusations. Their pinstripes pen an alphabet of denial that tastes sharp like a lid closing. The part in his hair moves above her. His hair is a quiver of arrows pinning needles through her skin. A row of tidy suits is an order. A passport is a fire that heats the drawer in his desk.

318 Her hands ache. Light runs from them, streaming out like sick bees from a hive. They sting yellow and black. She opens her mouth. There is silence where a buzzing should be. His head leans against the ring of the tub. The blade in her hand is a blade of grass. The air from her throat empties with the water running down the drain.

319 The hunter has a heartbeat the deer no longer hears. The deer lowers her head to eat. A slow rain falls from the hunter's breath. Heartbeats map the puddles.

320 The target is a body filled with clouds of needles.

321 Expectation travels faster than a bullet from a .243 raised to accommodate its slight drift.

322 (Expectation has a wider reach than the target.)

atch the school

323 A broken cup is a bruised cloud.

324 The flat is an unfinished sentence.

325 Raising her eyes is a cinder; lowering her eyes, a tidal wave of bricks.

326 *Drip drip,* says the house, a carriage return.

327 *Tap tap tap,* taps the baby.

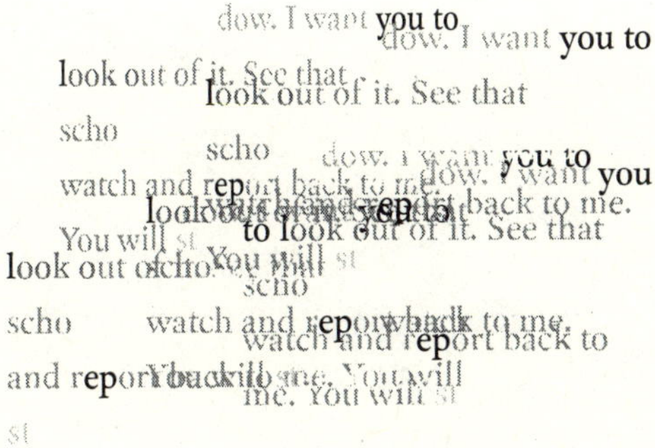

328

328 A window overlooking a schoolyard can be an unpunctuated sentence. If she doesn't look, will the children disappear? Will the window become a windshield wiper? Can five steps equal zero schoolyard satchels? She releases words that set two places at the table. Spoons gathering sighs allow 323 breaths.

329 Omissions are not an emptiness. There are multiple ways to tangle several threads but only one way to untangle a mouth.

330 (Sometimes memory ordered, and reordered, is an unordering.)

331 Sometimes there are no answers. The answer is worse than the bullets, which are his fingers. Sometimes a baby should not be born where it germinated.

332 A word held in the throat is a worm. She feels the worms with their tiny muscular mouths migrating through her flesh. In the night her hands move over the skin, looking for exit holes.

333 The shoes by the door are a sign. She counts the shoes. 1, 2, 3, 4, 5. Six is a loss. She lines up the shoes alphabetically. She places pebbles in each mouth. She holds her tongue, a dictionary of flattened braille. 1, 2, 3, 4, 5, 7. Holds their tongues. The laces are unthreaded words. Tie them up. Tie them up. Tie them up.

334 She leaves prints on the wall that map the fall of a bird shot from the sky.

335 Shoe my buckle

336 Three. Three. Three.

337 There are 337 steps between the front door and the top of the hill. She opens her mouth to the other passing birds. Silence is the distance between an open mouth and a bird's stretched wing.

338 A good girl is allowed 347 steps. Her legs are weak passages. The furrow between her legs with its small, dammed lake is sinking into the grassy hill. If her body is planted, will he write to all the blocked addresses? Can she crawl through the earth?

will carry this at a 339

339 She grows extra ears and eyes that prickle along her skin. Is an opening door a closing window? The weight of a mobile is not mobility but a thread that follows her up the 243 steps of a green hill.

340 Cut strings sometimes rise like rhizomatic tendrils to spread forgotten thoughts. She unearths words with the apple corer. Her thoughts are cut into bite-sized pieces.

341

341 She listens quietly enough to hear two heartbeats pulsing like stars talking through trees. Ribbons of aurora float over her half-moon belly.
342 Her head on the wall is a nodding sky, nausea a rotting apple. He holds her up on the pillow. Between his breaths, she floats her thoughts through the window so they do not thread into his hissed warnings. Sometimes three heartbeats do not balance six arms and six legs.
343 Will pound notes exchanged for a pound of butter and a bottle of red sauce burn holes in a bear?
344 Sometimes a plan is a simple omission. Sometimes a plan is a stuffed bear. How many pounds collect from quarts of milk? Her breath is a footfall.

345

345 If she stirs his tea with 2.5 revolutions and grills two slices of bread with cheese at 350° for 4.5 minutes while the cheese raises eight browned bubbles, and she holds her breath for five beats, will her eyes turn blue like his and see the order that is an approved map?

346 Her skin is a circuit board that conducts shifting signals. She is a conduit for the electricity of a changed breath. A calculus for the weight of a footfall.

347 *Tap tap,* says the man.

348 A cell is an ear.

349 Can she stuff her belly with vowels and leave all the consonants writhing on the floor? Will she be able to raise her arms to hold a baby after the birds are in orbit? Will she root to the floor and not fly into the snapping pre-storm sky?

350 She eats her cereal more quietly and swallows sentences that sprout twenty-four Canada geese flying in the formation of a consonant that is not her victory. The toast burns. Her words migrate. Will the door open on a Saturday morning? Will green grass race down the hill?

351 352

351 Good girls get a walk.

352 A walk can be a tangle. A walk can be a swing that imprints chain links. The hill is a return. If she closes her eyes, the grass under the checked skirt is a runway. If the silver chains bruise the eyes and leave fingerprints in the shape of a swing, will the checkered sky rain daisy chains? If she closes her eyes, she will not see.

353 354

353 Continuous motion is inertia until a force slows a woman's tongue.
354 The scent of metal is dried blood.
355 (The time it takes for legs to make their back-and-forth movement depends on the length of the sentences.)

s like this, h 356

357

356 If she closes her mouth, her eyes will not open.
357 If she stirs the pudding fourteen times counterclockwise, he will not see.
358 The girl will not see returned footfalls. The seeing is a slivered cloud. It tips water she cannot hold. Her hands are burning sieves.

es, yes 359

No, no 360

I am sorry 361

Not sorry 362

Yes you 363

Yes 364

359 He has studied the book in which a woman follows the man's threads, in which the only possibilities are hard lines.

360 The skin is an envelope of eyes that never close.

361 What she does not see he does not require her to translate.

362 She shutters her eyes. Each eye is a window.

363 What is deliberately unseen and that which is required to be seen measure how much moonlight is separated from morning.

364 *Yes, yes.*

365

365 Her skin is folded into his arms, a printing press. The cake she has baked has not been spliced open. The cake is a hive of bees. The guests stand together in the kitchen. Behind their open mouths, tight bubbles float toward the kitchen ceiling. She is an inarticulate poppet, a spinning bobbin with no thread. She is falling up into hailstones.

366 What she must articulate does not balance what she cannot articulate. Is the mistake words spoken openly or words protectively withheld?

367

367 A swing is an exposure she cannot splice.
368 Sight is an imprint. Ribbons of celluloid flicker behind the eyes.
369 If she blinks only twice in a minute, her eyes will expose only two seconds of motion; a swing will return to the sky. If she blinks her eyes forty times in a minute, they are not closed.
370 This equation does not include terms for the mass of the consonants or the length of the park through which the pendulum swings. The only factor that significantly affects the swing of a pendulum on earth is the length of its sentences.
371 How much swaying back and forth can a woman withstand before her throat closes? (Blinkered eyes are broken sentences.)

dren. You will watch them every

d tell me what dren. You will watch them every

dren. You will watch them every

d tell me what you see. dren. You will watch them every

d tell me what you see. You will start

d tell me what you see. You dren. You will watch them

every d tell me what you see. You will start

t

372

372 If the children run into the school unseen, will he allow one or two visits to the midwife? Will four hands count to twenty? Will eyes open? She sprouts a skein of fluttering purple wings. The baby taps only three times within twelve hours inside the tight drum.

373 *Chirp, chirp,* chirps the baby bird.

374 Purl one.

375 Drop one.

376 The sounds that unfurl from her throat fall on deafened fingers.

377 What must not be spoken is a closed map.

378 *If it's a girl.*

379 (Some things cannot be spoken, even in an empty room.)

If it's a boy you will have an abortion.
If it's a boy you will have an abortion.
If it's a boy you will have an abortion.
If it's a boy you will have an abortion.
If it's a boy you will have an abortion.
If it's a boy you will have an abortion.
381

380 She counts heartbeats. There is an inverse relationship between the number of taps and the number of days. There are forty-six steps around the perimeter of the flat. Thirty days before a credit card summary is delivered.

381 *If it's a boy.*

Each word is a larva she stirs into the batter.

She can't name the threads that spool from an X chromosome.
The weight of one does not balance the weightlessness of the other.

The deer and a gestating baby listen like a midnight sky.

If it's a girl, the two of you will show me adoration.
If it's a girl, the two of you will show me adoration.
If it's a girl, the two of you will show me adoration.
If it's a girl, the two of you will show me adoration.
If it's a girl, the two of you will show me adoration.

390 She closes her words in drawers. The drawers are mouths with sharp teeth. Her fingers bloom petals of blood where she squeezes out the slivers, which are not wood but the emptied carcasses of pantry worms.

I will take her I will take her I will take her I will take her I will take her I will take her I [391]

[392]

391 In the bush three deer and a fawn take twelve steps.
392 She threads one thousand moths, which are mouths, to a tree from which apples intermittently fall.

393 Apples jiggle in boxes in the box of a pickup. A 4 x 4 with a threaded track bumps over half-frozen mounds of dirt. Spruce branches brush against the jacket of a hunter crouched under the trees. There are 2,547 steps between the hunter's truck and the flattened grasses where the deer slept. A hard frost melts on the cooling hood. The hunter leaves his prints in the hoarfrost raised above the wet earth. The deer duck under low branches. Their criss-cross tracks are a map that can only be read in relief. The tracks of birds are threads that don't need untangling.

O

394 A hunter jiggles to revive his cold and numb limbs. Worms tingle through his flesh. His breath is a bite. Will a baby floating in its warm sac, with ears opening to sound, look up when the hunter raises the gun to his shoulder and says a short prayer under his breath?

395 A grouse, startled, is a gunshot.

396 The hunter exhales, the deer exhales. Blood blooms on leaves. Apples tart.

397 A mouthful of cloud translates into vapour.

398 The hunter lays a hand on the still-warm belly of the deer. His words spin upward, edit dew. The hunter splices the warm belly with its blue-veined sac.

399 She holds a handful of earth.

400 A field dressing is lighter than a changing room. The hunter dresses the deer. In the dusk, light flies away.

401 In the yellow room, the mother undresses the baby. Their skin is warm as they float together in the bathwater.

402 The hunter's hands are warm in her blue blood. The milk under the blue-veined skin of the doe slips down her belly in white-blue lines.

403 The baby inches toward her mother's scented breast and draws threads of milk. The baby climbs on her mother's chest and suckles her nose. The woman sniffs the baby's head.

404 (Sometimes the only certainty is the sense of smell.)

4:05

405 When the deer drops to the ground, her black eye reads the closing sky. Dark closing, dark opening.

406 When the twinned lungs of a doe are hung in a tree for the birds on a Tuesday evening at dusk, does a house breathe? Will four or eight birds feast? When a deer's heart is tenderly removed and carried in a blue bowl with an onion round and white like the moon, will a house form a tapestry of clear sounds? Will a mother's milk become a blue thread? When the kidneys of a deer are eaten by coyotes at midnight, a house opens its windows and breathes birds for the moon.

407 A cake browns in an oven at a house with one apple tree. The last apple drops from the tree on Wednesday at 4:05 a.m.

408 Silver threads thunder. The alphabet reorders.
409 She has walked twenty-seven steps from the locked door to the bedroom 1,425 times since the baby was born.
410 Sometimes a locked door is an open room. Sometimes when a woman's breath and the breath of the baby meet in the air, and the air is cool and purple, there is a fluttering of wings.
411 When she stays in the bathwater until the water is cool and the gold light seeps into their flesh, the words under her skin slide down the drain with the small vortex of water churning down the pipes.
412 When a neatly wrapped bundle is a venison roast, and a door opens on a honeyed garden, words thread out of her mouth.

413 The deer has hung in the cool air for nine days.
414 The hunter sees her hands moving but doesn't remember how many crystals of ice collected between her fingers.

Take it, he says.

Zero, she may have said.

She walks twelve steps to the kitchen.

Six, five, four, three, two, one.

Zero is a mercy.

415 Ten fingers sometimes equal ten.

0

416 An empty swing, its seat open to the sky, is an exhalation.

(Sometimes a swing is a swing.)

The hunter rises from his warm bed and drinks coffee.

The hunter's reflection grows until the sun opens the window like thought.

The hunter drizzles two spoonfuls of strawberry jam, made when the deer were fawning, onto two slices of warm toast.

The small wild berries are constellations of red stars in green grasses.

The mother cooks venison in a black skillet.

When the mother softens onions in a black skillet and doesn't count to ten while the baby pushes through her first tooth, and the meat is warm and scented with onion and rosemary, vowels and consonants sometimes form into a bushel of words.

At dawn the deer raise themselves from their beds under the cedars and in the grassy fields. The earth is a dressed hand.

The deer thread their tracks through the woods. The meandering lines remain, even when the deer gather in the wintering yards. The trails criss-cross under the needle tracks of planes. The threaded maps trace the dirt and mud under the melting snow.

The baby crawls backward down the stairs and claps at the bottom.

The baby's toes are round moons. Each reaching toe of a baby crawling down a flight of stairs is a wish and a certainty.

Clap clap, claps the baby.
Clap clap, says the mother.

She folds the baby in her arms and raises stars to the monarchs lifting off for migration.

The still hour before dark and dusk is a basket of berries.

Silence can be a cup.

She lies on her belly in a room that is an arcade of flying light. She lays her belly, which is a belly, on the floor. Her belly is not a debt but a basket of consonants and vowels.

Her fingers, spread open, catch the word-seeding clouds.

Interpretation is a spread hand.

Her words are migrating butterflies, a dozen hummingbirds.

Bees suckle sentences from the apple blossoms. She stirs stingers into her tea. Swallows language. Swallows the small hard apple buds that spell morning.

A dozen jars on the counter release the air that weaves through the cooling sauce. Threads of light are suspended in the honey.

The light spilling from the window fills her hands.

Sometimes light can be a set of shears.

Snip, snip, says the mother.

On Monday the mother spoons pink applesauce for the clapping baby whose pink mouth is a song.

Clap, clap, says the mother, who laughs and blows blue kisses to the singing baby.

She sings with the baby. Their budding vowels open and float to the ceiling.

She threads the fingers of each hand in her lap.

Mama, mama, says the baby.

Yes, yes, says the mother.

ACKNOWLEDGEMENTS

For all those folks who worked quietly in the background so I could write and publish this book—you're my main page people!

Thank you, Stuart Ross, for including me in this incredible series of books, and to Guernica for supporting Stuart's 1366 adventure, and mine.

JackPine Press published an excerpt in a gorgeous limited-edition chapbook under the title *Footnotes*. Cameron Anstee helped me troubleshoot the design and did a beautiful job with the layout. *A Mouth of Vowels* was longlisted for Omnidawn Press's 2024 1st/2nd Book Award, judged by Desirée Alvarez.

Richard Froude offered a wonderfully stimulating workshop on experimental and hybrid forms through Lighthouse Writers—the first pages of this book came out of that experience. Funding from the Canada Council for the Arts gave me the time to develop those early pages into a full manuscript.

Several residencies and retreats made all the difference: the Al Purdy A-Frame Association; the Banff Centre for the Arts Winter Writers Program, where I was fortunate to work with Souvanhkam Thammovongsa and Mónica de la Torre; and Sage Hill, with Jordan Abel. Your encouragement meant the world.

My neighbour Phil Smythe mowed my lawn and did a myriad other chores during a particularly challenging summer so that I could save my two hours of daily energy to clack away at my typewriter.

I have unending gratitude for Delaney Campbell, who, with great skill and compassion, helped me unravel my own PTSD ribbons so I could wind typewriter ribbons instead. Ever grateful to Noojmowin Teg Health Centre for welcoming this zhaagnaashiikwe into their program; Lisa Stihl and Josh Eshkawkogan and many others continue to help me along the way.

sophie anne edwards was born and raised in Northeastern Ontario. She lives on Mnidoo Mnising (Manitoulin Island) with her daughter and various roommates that include a pack of dogs and other "WWOOFers." She gardens, writes, and keeps an eye out for sandhill cranes and sweetwater women. Her debut poetry collection, *Conversations with the Kagawong River* (Talonbooks), was a CBC Books "must read." *A Mouth of Vowels* was published in chapbook form as *Footnotes* (JackPine Press) and longlisted for Omnidawn's 1st/2nd Book Award. Her work has otherwise been published in *The Capilano Review, CNQ, Arc Poetry, periodicities,* and *Empty Mirror,* among other journals. She has also been longlisted for the CBC Poetry Prize, shortlisted for an Arc Poem of the Year, and won third place in the Hybrid Grain contest judged by Jordan Abel and Kate Sikloski.

About 1366 Books

1366 Books is an imprint of Guernica Editions, launched in 2024 to bring to light two books of innovative but accessible fiction annually. Each title—whether a novel, stories, or microfictions—is a unique literary experience. Imprint editor Stuart Ross welcomes submissions of fiction manuscripts that challenge or attempt to redefine the boundaries of the genre. He is especially interested in seeing manuscripts of experimental fiction from members of diverse and marginalized communities. Write to Stuart at 1366books@gmail.com.

2024

The Apple in the Orchard, by Brian Dedora

Strange Water, by Sarah Moses

2025

Furthermore, the Lake, by Michael e. Casteels

A Mouth of Vowels, by sophie anne edwards

1366Books

Exploding Fictions

MIX
Paper
FSC® C100212

Printed by Imprimerie Gauvin
Gatineau, Québec